'TIS THE SEASON

JK LARKIN

CONTENTS

CHRISTMAS TREE

LYNN WHITE

Trimming the tree each Christmas Eve

was my family's ritual.

My cousin would come to help my mum

carefully take the glass baubles from the box

that used to hold Topsy, her big doll.

Then they would put them all in their place.

"No, the elephant doesn't go there,

that's where the peacock should be

and the Christmas pudding goes above."

Everything had its place on the Christmas tree

in my family.

There were shiny miniature crackers

never to be pulled

and curly, coloured candles

never to be lit

for economy.

No cheating tinsel was allowed

only glass baubles should cover the tree,

hiding the green.

The baubles had belonged to my cousin,

so had the tree.

And earlier, to her mother and granny.

They were part of the family.

My cousin's husband used to say with some truth,

we were the only family to fall out over trimming a tree

as every year the arguments were replayed.

Then they drank Santa's sherry and ate his mince pies.

Must have needed them after trimming the tree

in my family.

CHRISTMAS PASSED

LINDA TROTT DICKMAN

For I know the plans I have for you, declares the Lord, plans to prosper you and not to harm you, plans to give you hope and a future. Then you will call on me and come and pray to me, and I will listen to you. You will seek me and find me when you seek me with all your heart.

Jeremiah 29:11-13

In my heart like a molten core,

burning always.

Gifts gathered, ordered, sent.

Minimal tree ornamentation,

a smattering of past, present, future.

Family gathered,

. . .

Not the food that was planned.

Not all the people that were hoped for.

Elements served:

linguine and clam sauce -

great batch, good sauce, happy bread

garlic frosted, warning any sickness

to clear out.

Services attended,

sung, cried through.

Return, wrap, repeat

wrap, repeat.

Will we ever find all the gifts?

Perfect day, again unplanned.

Love shared

Moms and Dads watching from beyond.

Baking bringing tears,

singing bringing tears,

pretty much everything bringing...tears

All of this, and I missed it.

Sitting here, on the edge of New Year's Eve

Plans canceled,

nothing about this year in my order,

and yet it is ordered.

WINTER'S FIRST MOMENT

LYONS MCBEAN

When the last of our leaves are fallen and raked,

and the last jack o'lanterns are carved and then baked,

when our t-shirts and shorts have been smooshed into boxes

replaced with red sweaters and warm fluffy sockses,

The first floof of snow with its quillions of friends

throws floof-floofing parties proclaiming the end

of one more grand year (it went by so fast!)

and turning our doorknob of one more year's passed.

The one time of year when younglings and onelings

quit iPads and phones and electronic funlings,

don parkas and glarkas and glawter-proof boots

and stare out the windows at winter's cold fruits.

Their heads filled with blizzards and candy and presents

of lights and snow angels and—did I mention presents?

And hoping that effort of sheer concentration

brings about the ultimate triumph: school cancellation!

And while enthralled younglings, their heads in the stars,

dream of dancing sugar plums (whatever those are),

the oldlings among us dream different dreams,

we dream of the theme of winter's great dream.

For winter's the moment when families all gather,

a twinkle of time when all of us rather

spend time with each other and not with ourselves,

which oldlings love better than reindeer and elves.

So the next time a floof brings a quillion or two

of its friends and its friends' friends to pile anew,

sure, put down your abacus and your calculator,

don't bury your face in a gluff-huffinator,

and just as you want to play in that snow,

just think for a moment, before you just go,

does my favorite oldling require a hug?

And hug hug your oldling until we're all snug.

For snugging's the thing that will make us all warm,

the simple-dimple thing that really transforms

the younglings to oldlings, a moment at least,

through love and through spirit, and gives us all peace.

MERRY CHRISTMAS EVE
(GRANDPA'S WALK)

LISA DIAZ MEYER

Scarf, hat and peacoat

Oversized mittens, restraints

A harsh workday complete

Merry Christmas Eve

"Grandpa's gone for a walk", the children say

Many hours ago

The scene: A frumpy living room

Where our tiny festive tree boasts its

Tawdry blinking lights

The paltry sum of Christmas cards

Must be magical tonight

On the avenue, the shops are closed

The streets are silent with snowfall

The churches are alive with prayer and song

"Grandpa will be back", I tell them

Merry Christmas Eve

STILL PROCEEDING

LINDA TROTT DICKMAN

I am moon glow on a quiet winter night.

I am the cheer in the luminaria that brightens your path.

I am the fervent shine in the Shamash, servant to all.

I am the glint in the tear that falls from a loved one's eye, remembering holidays past.

I am the brightness in the Christ candle.

I am the sparkle in the icicle that formed in that funny corner of the kitchen window.

I am the diamond flakes, illuminated by the dawn.

I am the star at the top of the Christmas tree.

I am the sparkle in the eye of that wee one who waits as you open a special gift.

I am the twinkle in your friend's smile.

I am the hope in the ball that marks the end of one, and the beginning of the next year.

I am light, ignited by love, fanned by joy, and burnished in this happy, holy season.

THE PRESENT

ANITA HAAS

On a cold white Christmas long ago

A friend gave me a present.

Ooh and *Ahh* I told him then,

"How kind, how sweet, how pleasant."

At once I started on my scheme

To pass the present on.

I had no use for this old junk

And it didn't take me long.

So soon I found my lucky chance

and gave it to a friend.

I thought I'd seen the last of it,

And that had been the end.

But little did I know it then

My friend would follow suit

And soon the gift was sent again

Along its merry route.

Round and round the present went

Passed along the chain,

Of family, friends, acquaintances

And back to me again!

CRUEL YULE

GARY WATKINS

Desperate to fill voids

beneath trees,

within stockings,

in children's hearts,

society's seconds,

scratch-and-dent people,

unemployed close-outs,

pick the bones of Christmas,

seeking salvation

in the clearanced,

discontinued,

and reduced-to-sell.

It's the thought that counts,

but the cash that's counted

when money's tight

as a hangman's noose.

Each trinket is wrapped

in bits of brightness,

with love and hope,

and a prayer that it's enough.

A KISS UNDER THE MISTLETOE

GRAY WATKINS

The boss had too much egg nog

at the office party. Oh,

She set her goal to snog

me beneath the mistletoe!

With lecherous intentions

she stalks me 'cross the floor

until she finally pins me

against the bathroom door!

Her boozy breath assails me.

I very nearly swoon!

Her scarlet nails impale me.

I realize I'm doomed!

The darting of her tongue

leaves me in a daze.

Her kiss, so thick with rum,

I better get a raise!

TEACHER'S REFRAIN

COLLEEN MOYNE

It's term four, final week

and everything's in chaos.

This is when we earn much more

than they can ever pay us.

The kids are going crazy -

they sure know how to play us

(Our job would be much easier

If they would just obey us!)

The end of year reports are due -

it's such a chore to write them,

we have to word them tactfully

so mums and dads will like them.

We mustn't write the awful truth,

'cos that would just incite them.

(This time of year, we haven't got

the energy to fight them.)

The kids are into Christmas crafts,

there's lots to make and do,

like little Santa faces

from a paper plate or two,

with cotton wool for whiskers

and pompom noses, too

(and everywhere I look right now

there's paint and tape and glue.)

There's glitter in the carpet,

there's glitter on my chair.

I never knew there could be

so much glitter everywhere!

I wonder - should I clean it up?

but I don't really care,

and oops - I've found more glitter

in my eyelashes and hair.

There's furniture to scrub and clean

and graphs and charts to take down.

There's parties in the classrooms

and the mums are bringing cake 'round.

The kids are filling pockets

and we'll have to do a shakedown.

(The office staff are just about

to have a nervous break-down!)

I'm counting down the hours now,

I'm counting down the minutes.

I'm trying to be patient

but I think I've reached my limits.

The siren sounds! Oh, sweet release!

I hear the victory in it.

The Christmas break is here at last

and I'm off to begin it!

AN AUSTRALIAN CHRISTMAS

COLLEEN MOYNE

Balmy summer evenings

and the lengthening of days

are telling us that Christmas

isn't very far away.

The kids are making Christmas crafts

at school with all their friends.

They're counting down the days until

another school year ends

Candy canes and tinsel

are appearing in the stores

Holly wreaths and ivy

are appearing on the doors.

The neighbor's stringing lights

around his fences and his yard.

The letterbox is filling up

with catalogs and cards

We're writing out our Christmas lists

and planning Christmas dinner.

The lists are getting longer

and the budget's getting thinner.

Carols sung by candlelight

are wafting on the breeze

with floating purple blossoms

from the Jacaranda trees.

And now the day is finally here,

the frenzied pace abating.

It's time to open presents up

and start the celebrating.

The barbeque is fired up,

the beer is set to chill.

There's jelly, fruit and ice-cream

so the kids can have their fill.

The relatives will gather there

to share the Christmas cheer

and too soon…it will be over

for yet another year.

BRIGHT NIGHTS

KATHRYN SADAKIERSKI

We are on this time-honored route

Through displays of incandescence,

The same seen in childhood,

When we packed the car

With cookies and cocoa,

Family,

Cheer blanketing us all,

As it does now.

This year, no warm glow of light

Spills from the gift shop

Where Santa would wait,

And those who greet us

At the opening gate

Wear masks,

Not holding print programs

As they used to,

Everything this year

Being digitized.

Perhaps we hold no papers

In our hands,

With photos of the memories

Gathered through the years,

But the songs of glad tidings

Still croon from the radio,

And at a time

When so much is online,

Intangible

Like ghosts of the past,

We can still drive through the lights,

Incandesced from within,

Living on, sustaining traditions,

On this time-honored route.

Skaters hold hands, and

The Victorian passengers

In the carriage,

On their trip to the present,

Carried by their faithful horses,

Carts bearing gifts and evergreen

Like Santa's reindeer,

Are reflected

In the pond,

Colors of their lights

Too brilliant,

Aurora borealis

Streaks of cray-pas in the water,

To be captured in the camera,

Prismatic shadows

Dancing in the ripples of time,

Ombre pools,

That coalesce into the stars' shine.

Snowflakes and reindeer,

Luminescent,

In crescent arches

Over the car,

Always leaping,

Always onward,

In loops

Towards their next destination,

Points on the map,

Twinkling like the Pleiades,

Belts of gems,

Carousel of blue and white,

LED strings

Like sapphire and pearl beads,

Still swirling.

If we measured all things

By what is lacking,

We would never see

All that is present,

Every blessing

To be thankful for,

On these bright nights

Of clarity and truth,

When so much beauty

Still surrounds

On this time-honored route,

Through the lights,

Through memories,

The pathways to our spirit

And these moments of realization

When we discover what matters

Is already with us.

THE GINGERBREAD BOY

JILL OCONE

The Gingerbread Boy

In his pointed hat of red,

His favorite,

Watched with the children

As the crowd counted down

From five with delight.

Then the lights came alive

And the star twinkled bright

From atop the town Christmas tree on Main Street.

The Gingerbread Boy

Accepted a red balloon,

His favorite;

He gripped its green ribbon

As it danced in the air,

The chorus sang about snow

While tiny flakes swirled

In the glimmering glow

From the town Christmas tree on Main Street.

The Gingerbread Boy

Climbed into the red carriage,

His favorite,

The clippity-clop

Of the horse's feet

And the jing jingle-jangle

From its bridle of bells

Rang out as the horse turned about

Near the town Christmas tree on Main Street.

Sirens suddenly screamed

As the parade of red fire trucks,

His favorite,

Arrived with

The jolliest of guests

Perched high on the roof.

He climbed down

From his ladder roost

Next to the town Christmas tree on Main Street.

He belted a joyful "Ho Ho Ho!"

The big man in red,

His favorite,

And winked at him...

The Gingerbread Boy.

His twinkly eyes awed

With wonder and delight,

He became a believer that night

By the town Christmas tree on Main Street.

ALL AWASH IN CANDLELIGHT

BRANDY LANE

I want to write of last Christmas Eve,

but how do I properly capture

the moment burned into my memory?

Oh, to wander back in time one year!

The candles lit, the lights dimmed,

and all I could focus on was you,

up in the balcony, in the soft glow.

If I were an artist,

I would paint that one moment.

. . .

You, just sitting there-- a masterpiece.

Your handsome face,

your hair,

you dressed all in black...

I had never seen you look more dashing.

I'm tearing up even now,

with the memory of how awestruck I was,

gazing up at you,

knowing I already had been given

one of the best gifts in the world

in knowing you.

I try not to lavish on you as much as I used to...

but those feelings never wane.

This longing always in my heart.

I refrain from many things I want to say,

but my darling... my heart still calls your name,

my mind still adventures always with you.

.   .   .

As bittersweet this decadence may be...

as I long for honeyed words

and milky glances

as you used to.

Time moves painfully fast,

yet achingly slow

for the anticipation that I have

that does not leave me...

I still can hold the mere magic

of those rare moments.

However few...

So intense and compact

that they still hold their power over me.

I don't wish this to ever end,

I don't wish to hide my feelings from you...

as it does nothing but torture my soul.

I had to write this letter,

because I had to clear my thoughts,

because every time I think

of Christmas Eve...

you will pop into my mind–

all awash in candlelight.

You took my breath away,

I tend to always find myself

having to remind myself to breathe...

even now, just thinking of you.

THE GRACIOUS BEQUEST

LUISA REYES

Just when goodness was left with no room
The flowers of earth did burst forth in bloom
With leaves that are red and shaped like a star
Poinsettias with beauty earth's drabness did scar.

For on the good night of Christmas Eve
The world was granted a longed-for reprieve
By the Rose of Sharon that conquers all thorns
With the truth and the light that are sharper than horns.

While wreathing the globe with the gift
That keeps all virtue from running adrift
Dear Jesus was born all wrong to annoy
Through the gracious bequest of life and joy.

HOLIDAY SPIRITS - A SELECTION OF POEMS

LINDA CRATE

- paper-thin wings of transcendent joy

mother says

Christmas will be

low-key

this year

I am ready to relax

after a taxing year

watching the lights

dance on the Christmas tree,

baking sugar cookies,

and watching movies;

snuggling into the warmth

of blankets and sharing

hopes and dreams

of what the new year

could bring—

I am ready to shed the

cocoon of this year

and become a beautiful butterfly

with paper-thin wings

of transcendent joy.

- I will search for the rainbow

I remember

new years

last year

we were all

hopeful

for a good year,

and I pray

this new year will

be better;

2020

is a vision that I know

we'd all like to put

in the mirror view

never to look back at again—

yet despite the challenges

this year gave us,

I will bask in the glow

of hope;

because sometimes before

the most beautiful rainbow

comes the most horrible storm—

and so I will search

for the rainbow

that burns away the stain

of this previous year,

and ushers in some light

for this coming year.

- why be a statue?

.   .   .

With every gift

I wrap

love and hope,

peace and compassion,

and I hope,

when they are unwrapped,

the warmth of these things

is expressed;

because I try to buy

thoughtful things for one to enjoy—

my one ex only brought

practical things

for people

as if joy were some

elusive thing he could not understand,

but I will never be that way;

I will give hope

and whimsy and laughter—

.   .   .

because life is meant to be

enjoyed and lived and felt,

- *Christmas brings*

As the snow

falls,

it glitters

like

diamonds

of hope;

and so I let

the pain

of the year

fall

in hopes

that one day I can

glow

like the beautiful snow—

. . .

Christmas brings

the joy of the unknown,

the togetherness

of family,

burning away the

lonely silence of long winter days.

- gift of the future

I always

miss our thanksgiving meal

because of work,

yet mother always makes me

a plate;

mashed potatoes

and gravy,

turkey and stuffing,

cranberry sauce

and pie—

I always feel guilty

that I have to work,

but I know

that Christmas is just

around the corner;

so I don't worry about it

too much—

because the gift of fellowship

is coming,

and I know that Christmas

is the most magical of all times;

where hope and dreams and magic

twine with kinship and friendships—

so I let the guilt slip away

to embrace the gift

of the future.

THIS IS DECEMBER

OBINNA CHILEKEZI

Laughter runs through the season, ahead

as marigold flowers smiles its way, with yellow teeth

along the bush paths, in this smiling season

A drunk

dressed in a festive mood staggers homeward,

strutting and smiling like the marigolds

A moony dog barks

at the drunk, and barks and barks

the drunk in a bleeding anger, responded

O'dog, o'dog, o'dog

if you drink what I drank

can you walk, can you talk, can you

all in the season

It's a season

mixed well with laughter and tales

and of the year's dying harvest,

and of the juicy gnomes

I have to go home,

this is December

Xmas is just in the air

12/11/18

CHRISTMAS MEMORIES

BRANDY LANE

Memories of Christmas's past

are present in my thoughts,

the dressing up, the candlelight,

the gifts that we had brought.

The garlands hung from church balconies,

while singing filled the air.

I shuffled through the hymnals pages,

quickly but with care.

The turkey was in the oven,

with stuffing on the side,

there was caroling, like "sleigh bells ring"

as we'd go for a ride.

The lights had all been carefully strung

on every house and tree.

Nativities were fashioned

with Kings on bended knee.

As far as thoughts, mine start to drift

much like the fallen snow

I think lovingly of family,

and the friends I've grown to know.

Like magic, snowflakes start to fall,

they dance on their way down

they land on everything in sight,

blanketing the ground.

I pray for them that Christmastime

will bring them all good cheer,

and pray for health and wealth for them

in the coming year.

THE NIGHT BEFORE CHRISTMAS – A CAMCORDER'S VIEW

STEPHEN DEWOLFE

Every so often, there are some new stories born
Of events on Christmas Eve, and the following morn.
The fables and lore have gone down into history,
But details of Santa remain a deep mystery.

People the world over have tried with all their might
To discover what happens on Christmas Eve night.
Then I heard this story, from a camcorder's view,
That answers, 'bout Christmas, questions old and questions new.

'Twas the night before Christmas, and all through the house
Several creatures were stirring: children, cats, a field mouse.
The family made sure I was set up and ready
With tape inserted, battery charged, tripod steady.

The stockings with much care by the fire were hung,
The tree lights were plugged in, and the tinsel all strung,
The ornaments and the creche were arranged just right,

As the family made ready for a silent night.

The children left a note, and some milk and cookies.
And carrots for reindeer (these kids were no rookies!),
Then they went off to sleep in some bed or other;
The house to be tidied by Father and Mother.

When the tasks were completed, they, too, wished to rest,
So they both settled down on the couch they liked best.
They talked as they looked up at the brightly lit tree
Of their Christmases past, and the one soon to be.

A busy day would begin with the next sunrise;
Mother and Father finally from their couch did rise.
Just the lights to unplug, and the fire to douse
Then it became truly quiet throughout the house.

I was fighting sleep but giving up in defeat
When I heard the sound of two (not so tiny) feet.
Who could it be? I sleepily wondered;
Then my lens cap popped off; my short rest was plundered.

My power was turned on, from my slumber I stirred;
Still, I saw not a thing, and I heard not a word.
Whoever had done this had done so from behind.
(I had to admire this enterprising mind!)

The footsteps then faded with their errand complete
To tape Santa in action - t'would be quite a feat!
For a while I did nothing but stare at the dark;
Looking at blackness is somewhat less than a lark!

Then, from above, I heard a soft thump on the roof;
It had to be Santa! But I waited for proof.
I heard a bell jingle, then a gentle command.

I guessed that the reindeer knew just where to stand.

Down the chimney, someone was coming from the roof.
The trip ended with a thump; a deep voice said "Oof!".
A man then stood up, without cuts, scrapes, or gashes,
Sneezed and said, "Someone should have cleaned out the ashes!"

It was too dark to see well, so I just listened;
He sprinkled stardust, after which the room glistened.
He was dressed all in red, with white trim and boots black;
With a twitch of his shoulder, he set down his sack.

The warm stardust glow showed a twinkling in his eyes
And made it clear that he was a man of some size.
His face was quite rosy with a fluffy white beard
And his wide grin made him not at all to be feared.

He read the quick note, of which the children were proud,
And ate his milk and cookies, and chuckled out loud.
He put the reindeer's carrots in his side pocket
Then went to the tree–put its plug in the socket.

He turned to the tree and saw the decorations,
Some old and some new, from both near and far nations.
Some had been crafted by hand, some from a store-bought,
All of them mounted with care and, clearly, much thought.

He saw bright colored balls, candy canes, and a dove
With the manger below, and an angel above.
Icicles reflecting the multi-colored light.
Santa paused; he was quite taken in with the sight.

Santa placed the presents all around the big tree,
On the rug, the couch, and on an antique settee.
He filled the stockings with so much chocolate and stuff

After checking they'd been hung securely enough.

His face was aglow with the joy of his giving,
And he wrote a message for all people living:
"Remember Jesus, family ties never sever,
And Christmas and I will surely live forever."

He completed his work without making a sound,
Then unplugged the tree and then took one last look around.
He heard my motor and glanced in my direction
And came to see in my lens his own reflection.

So this was Santa! The mystery now clear.
He folded his sack, again brought his face near.
He smiled brightly, as he whispered into my mic,
"Now, only you'll ever know just what I look like."

He smiled at me once again, then quickly he found
And pressed the right button; thus my tape he re-wound.
By doing so, he erased all image and thought
Of what Santa had looked like, and what he had brought.

After granting me another glimpse of his face,
He then tenderly snapped my lens cap back in place.
My eye was now covered; soon I, too, would sleep
To re-tape in the morning–his secret to keep.

"Ho! Ho! Ho!" I heard, "and thanks for the snack.
I've a long way to go, but next year I'll be back!
Just make your days merry; your future will be bright.
I'll relax tomorrow, once I get through this night!"

With no load to carry, he was quite light on his feet.
He sprang back up the chimney without missing a beat.
The snack for the reindeer, then from the roof the sleigh lifted;

With a click of the reins, into high speed, it shifted.

A good night, I thought, as the jingling sound faded.
How could one think of Christmas and then feel jaded?
I dreamt then of Santa, out there doing his thing:
The houses he would visit; the joy he would bring.

'Twas soon Christmas morning; not a creature was stirring
My tripod was steady, my motor not whirring.
Soon the children awakened and tidied their rooms
With excitement and laughter serving as their brooms.

At the top of the stairs they had one thing to say:
"Please, please", 'til they heard the awaited "O.K.".
Together, with parents, down the staircase they came.
(I recognized one set of footsteps, just the same!)

They paused when they saw me, then quickly rushed past
Right into the room, to see their presents at last.
My eye was opened, when my lens cap was lifted,
I saw presents and love: a family well-gifted.

BE THANKFUL

ROLANDA T. PYLE

Sometimes life can bring tears to your eyes

Yes, it can make you cry and have you sigh.

Life can be so very rough

Also very, very tough!

It seems like bad news comes in bunches

And all we can do is roll with the punches;

Because we know there's often a reason,

But most of all for everything, there is a season.

So we march on

So we pray on

So we trust and we praise

Trusting and believing that God has control of all our days.

So, this Thanksgiving, we give thanks and praise

For the good, the bad, and the ugly days.

We are alive and God has brought us through it all

And for those still going through trials, you too will stand tall.

So give thanks, give praise, and even sing

Songs and hymns–rejoice and let the praises ring

Out of your mouth and out of your heart.

Thanksgiving is always a great time to start.

LAST SUNDAY

VAUGHN ROSTE

Last Sunday, when I saw you last,

we laughed just like in days gone past.

I caught you up, we ate like kings,

you chided me for the same old things.

We parted on amicable terms,

our rapport strong and reaffirmed,

but back then little did we know,

at that time, not long ago,

that that was our last Sunday.

If I knew then what I know now,

I'd never leave so soon, I vow;

I'd want to talk more, hang, and play,

but that was our last Sunday.

I hope that now, where 'ere you be,

you hold fond memories of me.

I hope that, someday soon, you smile,

remembr'ing fondly, just awhile,

the fun we had last Sunday.

If I knew then what I know now,

I'd never leave so soon, I vow;

I'd want to talk more, sing, and play,

prolonging for just one more day -

perhaps to you my love convey,

and beg for one more Christmas day -

but that was our last Sunday.

THE FIFTEENTH OF DECEMBER

TUFIK Y. SHAYEB

Right around the fifteenth

of December,

you'll drain all the Collins

from your World's Best mug

and reach for the Ezra Pound

on the top shelf

later, you might even get

a little Plathtered

and just about then,

you will feel

like a Christmas ornament

with no tree,

or a neatly tied ribbon

with no present.

DECEMBER TWILIGHT

JOHN GREY

Skaters take one more spin

around the park pond,

before unbuckling their blades

in twilight shadow.

The tobogganist coasts downhill,

then drags his sled home

across packed snow.

A man and his malamute

leave their last sidewalk prints

before trudging indoors.

. . .

One light flicks on

and a second, a third respond.

First inside the houses,

then, in a chorus of green and red,

shine skips giddily up and down wires

that cling to fences, trees, fences,

and reindeer on rooftops,

One small luminous street

casts a soft gauze

on the moon.

THREE POEMS

S. RUPSHA MITRA

- Again, Winter

Calcutta breathes of Christmas lights and phenomenal sights of

 dew – mussed glow, seeping through the bony holes

 of our uncanny cornered emptiness.

The wind touches the card palace of truant escapes,

 as a soft soprano tune of pain, meaningfully sorrowful yet mellow.

The sky turns a pink grey every day, as the slow gentle

 fading out of lush spring memories, turning

 a black grey blur, petrifying as stone.

 And the yearning to be touched by the

muddled security of warmth grows, grows, uncontrollably more.

. . .

- A Calcutta Christmas

It is again that season in Calcutta,

The bony winters vivacity brushing through

Our scarred lives

Offering the exotic wisdom of resilience in the domes

Of our myocardial skies.

Again, it is winter, enough for

The Flury's shop to be lit

Up in Christmas light,

Hogg Market serenely undulating

In embellishment of moonstone white

And red, and

The endless warmth of soft mulmul shawl

To wrap us in sheaths

And layers of almost an

Eternity of sluggish, iridescent remembrance

How this cunning frisson,

Boiling broth

Of Nostalgia repeats itself

Every time, summoning us towards

Its inevitable chill,

Only to vanish suddenly in

The chaotic hustle of the mangy labyrinths,

Humming in the dungeons of hidden corners,

Inviting the efflorescence of spring.

- Those Holidays

It is back again, that shudder of thorough thoughts – the pooling quagmire of nostalgic retrospections, the holidaying happiness in the midst of winter shirr and silence.

I remember how it was – days of school picnics, trips of vacation, the dumb luxuriant fantasies of our Christmas, we were young girls

And young boys still thirsting for a quest, pilgrims in collecting clamps of fun to be restored in the enlarged Almirah of stack boxed, ironed memories.

I remember, the broth of coffee smell still moving me in the effervescent warmth of childhood comforts, still opening up the hearts of sturdy shells, gemstones of tokens, Christmas bells, stars unveil – like pearls cracking open from winter –

Taking us back to winter seasons lost in the mirage of molten moon-grey past.

THE ROSE ON HER TOMBSTONE

KATHERINE ABRAHAM

Lost was I
That Christmas night
Tired and forlorn
The cold seared through
The closer I drew
A Red Rose still glistened
On her tombstone.

A tear rolled down
As I blew on
Another wisp of snow
My heart whispered softly,
Darling, will you be mine
Today and Tomorrow?

Yesterday is gone
And so are you
The Rose now dons
A sorrowful hue

Try as I may to forget
My heart wants you,
Only You

In the distance
The church bell rings
Hallelujah! the choir sings
And then I remember a hearse
Memories of a death knell
Oh I wish I had told her once
Just once
Before she left me here in hell

The Battle of Belonging
You have now won
The War of Pride
My heart long lost
No darling
Don't leave me to fend alone
This cold Christmas frost

Time have I
But with you
Now None
I confess Darling,
I always, always knew,
You were the One.

I now watch
The dew roll off
Like the last tear
That left your eye
When on Christmas
Like every time you'd tried

You smiled and whispered
I love you, Baby,
Goodbye...

A PANDEMIC CHRISTMAS

MELODY LIPFORD

51 weeks of struggle, sacrifice, and surrender.

Surrender to new year plans of

Travels, weddings, graduations, ceremonies

In-school classes, in-person working.

Front line health care workers along with other

Essential workers kissing their loved ones

Before facing the uncertainties that lie ahead.

Past perceived priorities shifting

Steering directions from mass ascension to

Essential survival.

A humbling hallmark of human hope and grit.

Reforming, revising definitions of competitive success to

Unity and Resilience.

Approaching the remaining weeks and

Entering the holiday season

Reflecting on past Christmas traditions.

Reminiscing and realizing what was is not what

May be during a Pandemic Christmas with shopping, events,

and mass consumerism.

No, with a Pandemic Christmas there is

a weakened economy, a weakened ability for

some to purchase perceived perfect presents

For material consumption.

However, during a Pandemic Christmas,

There is a strengthened ability to appreciate,

What one has whether friends, loved ones,

A roof over their head, food in their pantry,

Toilet paper stocked in their bathrooms,

Jobs, if you're fortunate to have one, whether in-person

Or working from home.

Shoes on your feet, down to the most basic need of

Breath in your lungs.

.   .   .

No, a Pandemic Christmas is about much more

This year then scoring Cyber Monday deals

And beating the online or in-person competition

To purchase the perfect present.

A Pandemic Christmas is about being present

With our loved ones however we can

Whether in person, video chat, or even taking the time

To write a nice letter by hand.

A Pandemic Christmas is for making

Room for new perspectives of humble

Appreciation and gratitude.

Recognizing privileges and blessings in your life.

Helping those who have less, however you can.

Instead of focusing on new possessions you don't

Need or have room for inside...

A house that others may not have

With food you can share with families

While some may not have enough for their children

To eat this Christmas.

Imagine the love and kindness one can spread

Instead of harboring negativity and

complaining, filled with dread.

It's not how much you have that makes

you the happiest.

Sometimes it's helping our neighbor that

can bring out our shared humanity.

And reignite strength, love, and unity.

A Pandemic Christmas might not be

What one has imagined.

Maybe a pandemic can push new

Perspectives of kindness and love

In a time where needs are the new wants

For so many.

A Pandemic Christmas.

ANTICIPATION

JOHN M. FLOYD

On Christmas Eve

At noon I say,

"Ma, I can't *wait*

Another day."

"Why, sure you can,"

She says. "Here, take

Your pa another

Piece of cake."

"Excited?" he asks,

Forking hay.

He stops to eat;

"Can't wait," I say.

That night we ride

The wagon down

The hill to go

To church in town.

When we get home

It's cold and late;

In bed, I think:

I just can't wait.

And now it's time—

The rooster crows,

The floor is cold

To my bare toes.

The dark is no

Cause for alarm:

The sun's not up

Yet, on the farm.

Ma says, "So you're

Not sleeping late?

I grin and holler:

"I can't wait!"

Then Pa, in boots,

Comes stomping in

And says, "You'll have to,"

With a grin.

"We've cows to milk

And eggs to gather—

Can't postpone it,

Though I'd rather."

So once more I

Am forced to wait

Before the chance

To celebrate.

But finally there

It is: the tree,

With lights and gifts—

And some for me!

.   .   .

And later, when

It's done, and we're

All still aglow

With Yuletide cheer,

I sit with Ma

And Pa awhile,

And have a thought

That makes me smile:

With patience,

We appreciate

That things are often

Worth the wait.

MR. ROBOT

TUFIK Y. SHAYEB

you came home to us

pocket full of dying batteries

we did not know what to make

of it; your eyes–dim bulbs,

stoplight green and blinking

a perfect robotic blink–a toy

there was a distortion in it,

your voice a faraway record

a worn tape in your chest

replaying the same *made-*

in-china sounds, entertaining;

a tiny gun in your tiny hand,

a joke, we were embarrassed

for you, turning red as Christmas,

Santa hats, and laser beams

WOULD YOU LIKE ONE?

COURTNEY MURRELL

Tantalized were those hundreds of tasting buds,

each one selfishly extending toward the glory of a new experience.

Sweetness filled the room as she pushed the platter at me–

"Would you like one?"

Hastily, I replied, "No, thank you."

I often turned away when I wanted a cookie,

when I wanted the sweetness of a new experience.

I am not worthy of this expression of love I would tell myself.

Reflection leaves a bitter taste in my mouth.

Saying no when I meant yes only ever denied me the sweetness of
giving in to my instinct.

This Christmas, I am worthy of love. I will say yes if offered a cookie.

THE GIFT OF CHRISTMAS

EILEEN M HECTOR

Trees all decorated,

Presents all wrapped up,

Mistletoe hung strategically,

Hot cocoa in our cup.

Marshmallows floating in a swirl,

Steam, rising high,

Listening to the echoes of Christmas,

Of all the years gone by.

 A snowman stands out in the yard,

With freshly fallen snow,

Bits of twigs stuck on his head,

Bringing the laughter we all know.

An icicle dripping from the roof,

A melt is on the way,

Slushy boots and scarves and gloves,

Left on the porch today.

Popcorn kernels in the pan,

In boiling oil they jump,

Bouncing off of one another,

Poppity, pop, bump, bump!

Thread them through the needle,

Add a cranberry here and there,

Hang them out for the winter birds,

Our bounty we will share.

Fresh oranges and cloves,

The fragrances fill my head,

Candy canes wrapped in peppermint,

It's time to go to bed.

Under the worn, wonderful quilt,

I secretly say my prayer,

That Santa will come when I am asleep,

And leave some presents here.

'TWAS THE THRILL BEFORE CHRISTMAS

J.S. MANNINO

(In the Style of Michael Jackson's "Thriller" with a nod to Clement Clarke Moore's "A Visit From St. Nicholas")

It's close to midnight and something jolly's circling the house

Under the moonlight, not a creature stirring, not even a mouse

You take a peak but the kids are still nestled snug in bed

They start to dream as visions of sugar plums dance inside their head

They're mesmerized!

   'Cause this is Christmas, Christmas night

   And old St. Nick is coming before dawns early light

   You know it's Christmas, Christmas night

   You've waited all year long

   For this listless, Christmas tonight, yeah!

. . .

You hear the hoof steps and realize that Santa has arrived

You rise to greet him, quickly wiping cobwebs from your eyes

You start downstairs but Santa takes the chimney in one bound

You see him there dressed in fur from his head to his foot

He's covered in soot!

> 'Cause this is Christmas, Christmas night
>
> No time left to worry who's naughty and who's nice
>
> Christmas, Christmas night
>
> You're hoping for the best on this sleepless, Christmas tonight!

Sleigh bells chime

As the Claus starts to finish his deliveries

There's no escaping the naughty list this time (he checks it twice)

This is the end of the line!

His eyes they twinkled, his dimples merry, mouth just like a bow

His face was wrinkled, but his beard was white as the driven snow

Now is the time for Santa to fill up all the stockings

He finished his work and laid a finger aside his nose

Up the chimney he rose!

'Cause this is Christmas, Christmas night

Santa Claus delivers while we're nestled in quite tight

Christmas, Christmas night

Away he flew on his sleigh, with quickness for Christmas tonight!

Claus is coming tonight…

Darkness falls across the land

The yuletide hour is close at hand

Children slumber and dream of fun

As Santa down the chimney comes

And you, quite clever in your evening gown

Catch a glimpse of St. Nick making his rounds

(It's Christmas tonight!)

Stockings hung with such care

Old St. Nicholas was already there

The shelf-less elf chased away the gloom

Leaving Christmas cheer in every room

And oh yes he did exclaim

Ere he drove out of sight

A thrilling Christmas to all, and to all a good night!

ST. LUCIA OF WICHITA

AMY BARNES

There's no IKEA in Kansas

or playing with matches

except when a fragile flat-pack angel carousel emerges

from Christmas purgatory,

Attic storage, announces it's the holidays with tinkling puzzle pieces.

My sister and I are tasked with building slight wings

from buried wood that Smokey the Bear would warn against

Only you can prevent forest fires

doesn't apply to smoking angel decorations

or St. Lucia crowns, flammable flannel pajamas

and Advent wreaths with pastel candle celebrations

that look like candy but stand for *Joy, Love, Peace, Fire.*

Jesus will protect us from fire, he saved himself

in a wood box in straw and hay

but not on a wood cross where he wasn't allowed matches.

We walk in the fiery furnace of recalled bubble lights,

duct-taped extension cords

and remnants of a pine tree forest, sap dripping

Close, close to a Bear and matches and spinning chimes

that announce Jesus' birth

with finger white candles.

It is my year to light them all.

I close my eyes and make a wish,

pine branches and virgin candles heavy on my scalp.

ADVENT

DEBBIE DE LOUISE

A time to reflect
Be at peace
while the world rushes by

A time of prayer
Be enlightened
as the darkness descends

A time to believe
Be faithful
while hope slips away

A time to question
Be thoughtful
as answers elude

A time to grasp
Be open
while holds are heavy

A time to wonder
Be quiet
while noises invade

A time to reflect
Be at peace
while the world rushes by

Advent

LAST WALK HOME FROM SCHOOL

DAVID LANGE

Anxiously fidgeting, furiously scribbling

Doodles upon the page

Barely listening, second hand ticking

The clock owns the key to our cage

School bell now ringing, the children all singing

Holiday songs as they dress

While boots are now buckling, the teachers are chuckling

Forgiving their young pupils' mess

Parting words said to Jeff, Jim, and Ed

I sprouted some wings and I flew

But once in the snow, I just had to throw

A holiday snowball or two

Ouch! One in the face, freezing the place

Where it struck me just over the eye

Principal alerted; the school yard deserted

We ran as we shouted goodbye

Glistening alabaster, the snow falling faster

I purposely slowed down my pace

Fulfilling my duty to admire nature's beauty

There was no need to make this a race

Soon walking alone, I started for home

Down a path framed by snow-covered pine

Reveling as I go, privileged to know

That the very first tracks would be mine

Enjoying the breeze, I throw snowballs at trees

Only stopping when I hit five or six

Then nearing the pond, that lay just beyond

I gather some stones and some sticks

Throwing rocks way up high in the pale winter sky

I eagerly await their return

I'll hear either a rock-on-ice smash or a watery splash

Upon re-entry, the verdict I'll learn

The water's frozen today so the sticks go away

I slide stones from near shore to far

I wander about when my ammunition runs out

I am happy with things as they are

With freezing numb feet, I return to the street

The cars splashing slush as they pass

I get a bit wet but never upset

No, not on the last day of class

Up over the ridge, I soon cross the bridge

The sign for my village ahead

I'm now moving fast, my patience won't last

I neglect to watch where I tread

I soon pay the price on a cruel patch of ice

I fall back and land on my rear

It seems I'm okay so I get on my way

Thank God my mother's not here

· · ·

It's a sure bet she'd worry and fret

Had she seen me fall to the ground

But she's three blocks away and I'm thankful to say

She'll never know I was downed

Now feeling the chill, I ascend one final hill

Stepping aside for a plow

Taking greater care yet, since it's a fair bet

That my mother is watching me now

Up the driveway I go, through unshoveled snow

My mother's beautiful smile now in view

She races for the door, across our white tiled floor

And greets me just like mothers do

It's been a long walk, I'm not yet ready to talk

I just say the day went okay

But when I see our big tree something comes over me

And I feel like dancing away

There'll be Christmas shows on TV and hearts filled with glee

My sister and I will make gifts

And if the snow is persisting, there'll be no resisting

Sledding down hills and snow drifts

We'll have small parties at night and Christmas tree lights

Joy and excitement on Christmas Eve

Santa will come, before it's all done

My sister and I we believe

This all lay ahead after some more nights in bed

Boots and coat must come off first, as a rule

Not a morsel of grief, I sigh with relief

I love that last walk home from school

NEEDLE IN THE CORNER

DAVID LANGE

I close my eyes; my world comes alive.

Trumpets ushering in the holidays as angels sing.

Roasted turkey waftings, only recently turned memory, replaced by cookies and cakes yet made.

Cloaked and ambitious, I navigate the oceans of shoppers.

I hear the clang, clang, clang of Salvation Army Santas and the jingle of coins deposited.

Cabs honking, seasonal favorites played by street performers, the City all aglow in festive holiday colors.

Prizes claimed, I return in secret.

Scissors, meeting little resistance, cut cleanly through rolls of festive paper.

Folding here and there, treasures concealed; tape dispensers and brown pasteboard rollers scattered like autumn's dying leaves.

. . .

Anticipation; excitement building, my children try to show restraint but their eyes betray them.

I remember that feeling of hope; the belief that somehow my dreams might be fulfilled on a day.

I knew better.

Good enough was always good enough.

I was happy with what was; never disappointed by what was not.

I wanted more for my children.

The displeased face of my wife spoke the words she could not—too much.

Who was I pleasing?

I'm not sure I knew.

I was trying to add magic in a world that denied it—for my children; for me.

Late-night shuffling; all rooms checked for signs of consciousness.

Green leaf bags emerging from hiding.

Silent and deliberate foot placement; hoping not a single floorboard might creak beneath my weight.

Flashlights shielded; gifts slowly removed and placed around a beautiful tree.

Lights of rainbow hue set afire, blazing with holiday cheer; the stage is set.

Wait; what have I forgotten?

A cookie on a plate is attended to with crumbs carefully left for the forensic investigators.

Flat ginger ale sipped and the job is done.

The silent Ninja returns, brushes his teeth, slides into bed with a shiver.

A few hours of sleep before the shuffling begins.

Muffled voices as child speaks to child; flashlight beams dance across the scene.

Who gets the big box? I can almost remember when this mattered to me.

We gather around the tree; the curtains are drawn open; the play begins.

Children create their own traditions, uniquely theirs—I am glad.

Each collects their gifts, building a box fort about them—strange but endearing; I admire the creativity.

Gift opening remains as I remember from my own childhood; a tradition passed on.

Youngest to oldest; Mom before Dad; each gift a gift for all.

Children look for approval to open the next; parents attempt to manage the pace.

Christmas songs play quietly in the background.

Our dog's attention is focused on tasty bribes; it seems to work.

He'll soon have gifts of his own, chosen by the children.

We all give.

We all receive.

We share the beauty of the day.

. . .

Gifting complete, there's a sense of relief.

Eggs fry, bacon sizzles, biscuits rise.

Children investigate gifts meriting additional attention.

I ready tools; my work is not yet done.

Breakfast, alas, a formality and a distraction.

Soon the savory aroma of roasting turkey shall return to our home.

Connect part A to part B using screw Y and clip Z.

Dollhouses take shape; robots spring to life.

There is peace amidst the chaos.

We are connected with generations long departed.

Snow falls, gently.

I feel loss and I don't know why.

Perhaps the crescendo was too grand? The fall back to reality too steep?

Yet I am satisfied; satisfied because my family seems satisfied.

But happy? I don't know.

I hope.

Christmas cheer extended; we try to make it so.

I look towards the new year; I'm the only one.

We have the party; it's preordained.

I look towards the new year; I'm the only one.

Children to bed; wife to bed.

I look towards the new year; I'm the only one.

California to Korea, England to Saudi Arabia, countless time zones—my year always ends in New York.

I tolerate the festivities; music I don't care for; celebrities I do not celebrate.

My eyes are focused on the clock . . . and on the ball.

I see myself, a child.

My watch ready for its annual setting.

My heart rate picks up.

Where music and media personalities have failed, the movement of time has not.

I am . . . inspired.

I do care.

I mourn the passing of time yet I am filled with the hope that comes from new beginnings.

I am filled with hope.

I open my eyes; that world dies, washed away by a tear.

An empty home.

The tree stood here.

The children sat there.

A thousand memories; ten-thousand; a million!

The moving truck pulls away.

I am alone.

. . .

My children . . . a thousand miles away.

My wife is free.

I am free but I am dying.

I will not die; not yet.

Spotless floors, spotless windows, spotless spots—I have done well.

I turn to go but I cannot.

Kneeling; I've missed something.

A needle in the corner, a gift from a Christmas pine.

I wipe the tears from my eyes as I reach to cleanse the scene of its only debris.

I pull back and I stand.

The needle in the corner remains.

Not a gift to those who come next but my statement to the universe.

I was here; we were here.

We knew love, fresh and green.

Love faded, brown, dry and dead.

Like the needle in the corner, we had our time, we faded, we are resurrected in memory.

Summer heat burns as I open the door.

I need not look back.

The needle remains.

MERRY CHRISTMAS, EVERYONE!

ROLANDA PYLE

It's the most wonderful time of the year.

Such a very special time when…

We celebrate the birth of Christ,

by giving gifts, having fun and doing everything nice.

It is a time for sharing,

And it is also a time for caring.

Time for family, friends and those we love.

Time to reflect on Jesus and His Father above!

Hustle and bustle as folks shop in the store,

Holiday parties at work on each and every floor,

Store windows are decorated and looking great,

It's the time to love everyone and not to hate.

Christmas songs playing everywhere you go,

Bitter cold weather and hopefully lots of snow,

Kids are off from school and having fun,

Adults shopping, decorating, cooking — can't wait till it's done!

It's the most wonderful time of the year,

Such a very special time when,

We focus on Jesus' birth, which is the reason,

For this special, wonderful time and season!

MEET OUR POETS

KATHERINE ABRAHAM

The Rose on Her Tombstone

Katherine Abraham is the Author of Silenced by Love and Some Days are Forever. An Indian Adventist, Katherine is a teacher by profession, with degrees in Law, Literature and Journalism. She writes poetry and prose for various online publications as well as Anthologies. She is also the host for a New Podcast Series entitled, Chasing Hope. Her fourth novel "Every Sunset Has a Story" is currently looking for a home. Her short story, The Great Controversy between Faith and Fear has been accepted by the Red Penguins Publications, USA, recently.

Also by Katherine Abraham

Silenced by Love

Yesterday Once More

Some Days are Forever

Every Sunset Has a Story

Connect with Katherine Abraham

www.chasinghopewithkatherine.com

www.katherinerabraham.com

Twitter- @Katie_abraham

AMY BARNES

St. Lucia of Wichita

Amy Barnes has words at a variety of sites including The New Southern Fugitives, FlashBack Fiction, Popshot Quarterly, Flash Fiction Magazine, X-Ray Lit, Anti-Heroin Chic, Museum of Americana, Penny Fiction, Stymie Lit, No Contact Mag, JMMW, The Molotov Cocktail, Lucent Dreaming, Lunate Fiction, Perhappened, Cabinet of Heed, Spartan Lit, National Flash Flood Day and others. Her work has been long-listed at Reflex Press (3rd place), Bath Flash Fiction, Retreat West and TSS Publishing. She volunteers at Fractured Lit, CRAFT, Taco Bell Quarterly, Retreat West, NFFD, The MacGuffin, and Narratively. She is nominated for Best Microfictions (Spartan Lit) and Pushcarts (101 Words of Solitude and Perhappened.) Her flash collection, "Mother Figures" is forthcoming in May, 2021 by ELJ Editions, Ltd.

Also by Amy Barnes

Mother Figures (May, 2021)

Clean Up On Aisle 5 (June, 2021)

Connect with Amy Barnes

Twitter: @amygcb

LINDA M. CRATE

Holiday Spirits - A Selection of Poems

Linda M. Crate's works have been published in numerous magazines and anthologies both online and in print. She is the author of seven poetry chapbooks, the latest of which is: the samurai (Yellow Arrow Publishing, October 2020). She's also the author of the novel Phoenix Tears (Czykmate Books, June 2018). Recently she has published three full-length poetry collections Vampire Daughter (Dark Gatekeeper Gaming, February 2020), The Sweetest Blood (Cyberwit, February 2020), and Mythology of My Bones (Cyberwit, August 2020).

Connect with Linda M. Crate

My Facebook: https://www.facebook.com/Linda-M-Crate-129813357119547/, my instagram is: ,https://www.instagram.com/authorlindamcrate/, & my twitter: https://twitter.com/thysilverdoe?lang=en.

DEBBIE DE LOUISE

Advent

Debbie De Louise is an award-winning author of 8 mystery novels and dozens of short stories of various genres. She is a reference librarian at the Hicksville Public Library on Long Island and a member of Sisters-in-Crime, International Thriller Writers, the Long

Island Authors Group, and the Cat Writers' Association. She lives on Long Island with her husband, Anthony; daughter, Holly; and 3 cats Stripey, Harry, and Hermione.

Also by Debbie De Louise

The five books of the Cobble Cove mystery series: *A Stone's Throw, Between a Rock and a Hard Place, Written in Stone, Love on the Rocks, No Graveyard Unturned* and three short eBooks featuring the Cobble Cove characters: *Celebrating Christmas with my Characters, Sneaky's Christmas Mystery* (the 2019 MUSE Medallion winner from the Cat Writers' Association) and *Sneaky's Summer Mystery*. Debbie has written a standalone mystery, *Reason to Die*, a romantic comedy novella, *When Jack Trumps Ace*, a medical thriller, *Memory Makers*, and a paranormal romance, *Cloudy Rainbow*.

Connect with Debbie De Louise

Website/Blog/Newsletter sign up: https://debbiedelouise.com

Facebook: https://www.facebook.com/debbie.delouise.author/

Twitter: https://twitter.com/Deblibrarian

Amazon Author Page: http://amzn.to/2bIHdaQ

STEVE DEWOLFE

The Night Before Christmas - A Camcorder's View

For the last half of his five decades as an IT professional, mostly as a project manager, Steve deWolfe has also been dabbling in poetry. Subjects of his more than forty poems have included life, love, and sports, with rhymes sometimes taking an unusual point of view. As a husband, father, and grandfather, the potential subjects abound. Steve can be reached by email at steve.dewolfe@gmail.com.

LINDA TROTT DICKMAN

Christmas Passed

Still Proceeding

Linda Trott Dickman has been writing poetry since her first sleep-away camp experience when she was ten years old. Linda is the author of *Robes, The Air That I Breathe* and *Road Trip*. Linda's poetry has been published on-line, in Pratik Journal and in several anthologies. She is the current coordinator of poetry for the Northport Arts Coalition (Northport, NY.), has taught poetry to children for over 35 years and leads a poetry workshop for adults at Samantha's Li'l Bit O' Heaven coffee house in East Northport, NY.

Also by Linda Trott Dickman

Robes

The Air That I Breathe

Road Trip

Connect with Linda Trott Dickman

https://libearyn.wordpress.com/

Facebook: Linda Trott Dickman

JOHN M. FLOYD

Anticipation

John M. Floyd's work has appeared in more than 300 different publications, including Alfred Hitchcock's Mystery Magazine, Ellery Queen's Mystery Magazine, The Strand Magazine, The Saturday Evening Post, and three editions of The Best American Mystery Stories. John is also an Edgar Award finalist, a four-time Derringer Award winner, a three-time Pushcart Prize nominee, and the author of nine books.

Also by John M. Floyd

RAINBOW'S END (2006), MIDNIGHT (2008), CLOCKWORK (2010), DECEPTION (2013), FIFTY MYSTERIES (2014), DREAMLAND (2016). THE BARRENS (2018), LIGHTEN UP A LITTLE (2020), and SELECTED STORIES (upcoming).

Connect with John M. Floyd

www.johnmfloyd.com

https://www.facebook.com/john.m.floyd2/

JOHN GREY

December Twilight

John Grey is an Australian poet, US resident, recently published in Soundings East, Dalhousie Review and Connecticut River Review. Latest book, "Leaves On Pages" is available through Amazon.

. . .

Also by John Grey

Leaves On Pages

ANITA HAAS

The Present

Anita Haas is a differently-abled Canadian writer based in Spain. She has published books on film, two novelettes, a short story collection, and articles, poems and stories in both English and Spanish.

Some publications her work has appeared in include Falling Star Magazine, the Tulane Review, the Zodiac Review, Terror House, Wink and Adelaide Magazine.

Also by Anita Haas

Creating Florinda, Make a Wish Sophie, Yo Fui una chica Bond

EILEEN M HECTOR

The Gift of Christmas

E M Hector lives in the Sunshine State. She is married, has two grown sons and three grandchildren. Her work has been featured in online blogs and published in print, in local newspapers, and in several anthologies and literary journals. She spends much of her time volunteering with the local orchid growing community.

Also by Eileen M. Hector

Chicken Soup for the Soul Christmas, The Florida Writer, Haiku Journal #64, Castabout Lit, How I Met My Other: Furry Friends, True Tails, Work of Hearts, Minnie's Diary: A Southern Literary Review, Where Does Your Muse Live?: Florida Writers Association Collection, Volume 10, Writers @ Work: Florida Writers Association Collection, Volume 11, The Purple Breakfast Review, Issue 5: Sound and Silence, Orchids , Poetry Leaves, Women in Clothes

Brandy Lane

All Awash in Candlelight

Having a background and education in musical theatre and dance, Brandy uses her experiences to get the reader to not only read, but to take them on a journey of the senses through her use of imagery. This mother of four uses colorful metaphors and analogies to help readers (as well as her children) try to relate to the topics in order to draw out emotion. She has dabbled with writing music and poetry throughout her life, but didn't start diligently writing until two years ago when a good friend, also a lover of words and music, inspired her. Her supportive husband of twenty years is constantly helping her to push her own boundaries and step out of her comfort zone.

Also by Brandy Lane

Where Beautiful Loves (Where Beautiful Inks)

Poetry 365 November edition (@rdw.world)

The Rise and Fall of Chimeras Seasonal (Ink Gladiator's Press)

Connect with Brandy Lane

https://www.facebook.com/wherebeautifullives/

https://www.instagram.com/wherebeautifullives/

www.wherebeautifulinks.com

DAVID LANGE

Last Walk Home From School

Needle in the Corner

Colonel David Lange was born and grew up on Long Island, New York. A graduate of the United States Air Force Academy, he served for 30 years as an Active Duty officer in the United States Air Force before retiring in 2018. Colonel Lange is a decorated combat veteran, and flew numerous combat, combat support, and humanitarian relief missions during his career. He was awarded the prestigious Institute of Navigation Superior Achievement Award in recognition of his life-long accomplishments as a practicing navigator. David loves sharing stories of hope and inspiration and, in 2020, he published his memoir, *Quest: My Journey Through La Mancha.*

Also by David Lange

Quest: My Journey Through La Mancha

Connect with David Lange

www.davidlangequest.com

MELODY LIPFORD

A Pandemic Christmas

Melody Lipford is a poet, writer, and junior editor based in Southwest Virginia. A first generation college graduate, Lipford earned her Bachelor of Arts in English Literature with a minor in Spanish from Emory & Henry College in 2019. Drawing many influences from her Appalachian heritage, Lipford strives to create poetry that embraces and celebrates the region.

Also by Melody Lipford

Calla Press Magazine: "Guiding Star"

Calla Press Blog: "As White As Snow"

2020 Winter Train River Poetry Anthology: "Nanny's Kitchen"

Connect with Melody Lipford

Website: melodylipfordpoetry.wordpress.com

Instagram: @melodylipfordpoetry

J.S. MANNINO

Twas The Thrill Before Christmas

Joseph Mannino is a Tampa Bay based poet who, at the tender age of nine, had a poem turned into a song and performed for the entire school. Every day since, he has chased the breakout success of "Roller Skates." He has recently had a poem published in the "Circle of Magic" anthology and has been working tirelessly on his personal webpage,

Manninoacid.com. In complement to his passion for writing, he loves to run, climb, and cook.

Also by J.S. Mannino

Circle of Magic- A WPC Anthology

The Beauty Within- The Red Penguin Collection

Connect with J.S. Mannino

Blog: www.Manninoacid.com

FB: www.facebook.com/ManninoAcid

LISA DIAZ MEYER

Merry Christmas Eve (Grandpa's Walk)

Lisa Diaz Meyer is a three time winner of Literary Titan's Gold Book Award, IPA's Distinguished Favorite Award, and Readers Favorite 5 Stars. She's also the recipient of New Apple Literary's Official Selection in Poetry as well as their Solo Medalist Winner in Short Story Fiction. Her second book, ALL ROADS DESTINED was nominated for a CIPA EVVY and her third book, ALL ROADS SHATTERED was nominated and is a Finalist for TopShelf Magazine.

Her poem "Merry Christmas Eve (Grandpa's Walk)" is based off her short story and stage play published in her book, ALL ROADS HOME.

Lisa lives with her family and rescue cat on Long Island's south shore.

. . .

Also by Lisa Diaz Meyer

ALL ROADS HOME: A Collection of Short Stories

ALL ROADS DESTINED: A Collection of Dark Fiction and Poems

ALL ROADS SHATTERED: A Collection of Dark Fiction Short Stories and Poems

Several short stories in *WHAT LIES BEYOND: Science Fiction Anthology* by Red Penguin Books & *I CAN'T FIND MY FLASHLIGHT: Horror Anthology* by Red Penguin Books

Poetry in *NASSAU COUNTY VOICES IN VERSE 2020* (An Anthology of Poetry by Nassau County Poets) & Poetry in THE BARDS ANNUAL 2020: A Poetry Anthology (The Annual Publication of the Long Island's Bards)

Connect with Lisa Diaz Meyer

Website: lisadiazmeyer.com

Twitter: @LisaDMeyer

Instagram: Lisa Diaz Meyer

Facebook: LDMeyerAuthorALLROADS

S. RUPSHA MITRA

A Calcutta Christmas - A selection of poems

S. Rupsha Mitra is a student from India with a penchant for writing poetry. Her work is published or upcoming in Hebe Poetry, Santa Fe Literary Review, Muse India, Fly on the Wall Press

COLLEEN MOYNE

An Australian Christmas

Teacher's Refrain

Colleen Moyne is a published freelance writer living in the lovely riverside town of Mannum in South Australia. She has won several awards for her poetry and has had poems and short stories published in over twenty different anthologies. Her first solo collection, *Time Like Coins* was released in January 2019 by Ginninderra Press.

Also by Colleen Moyne

Time Like Coins - Ginninderra Press 2019

Connect with Coleen Moyne

www.colleenmoyne.com

COURTNEY MURRELL

Would you like one?

Courtney is a Relaxation Therapist who offers mindfulness to her readers through poetry, short stories and feel good blogs! She reminds us that "We are never alone, and all that we seek is already inside of us."

Also by Courtney Murrell

Just Be - Poetry amid Pandemic

Hero (a memoir)

Love & Loss (the journey to positive self talk and body image)

Connect with Courtney Murrell

calmonpurpose@gmail.com

JILL OCONE

The Gingerbread Boy

Jill Ocone is a senior writer/editor for Jersey Shore Magazine and a high school journalism educator. Her work has appeared in Harness Magazine, American Writers Review (2020 and 2019 volumes), Art in the Time of COVID-19, The Sun, Everywhere magazine, Dow Jones Adviser Update and NJEA.org, among others. Jill lives at the Jersey Shore with her husband and enjoys traveling and making memories with her nieces and nephews.

Connect with Jill Ocone

Website: jillocone.com - Facebook and Instagram: @jillocone - Twitter: @jill_ocone

ROLANDA T. PYLE

Be Thankful

Merry Christmas Everyone

ROLANDA T. PYLE is a licensed social worker and has worked in the field of aging for many years. She is the author of the books—*Grandma's Hands*—a children's story book, *Finally*—a collection of inspirational poems; and the compiler of and contributor to *Beneath His Everlasting Wings*, a collection of devotionals.

Rolanda's creative writing has won poetry and short story awards .Her work has been published in religious and community newspapers, anthologies, and journals and featured in the 50in50 writing contests with the Billie Holiday Theater.. In April 2004, New York's Daily News named her one of the "100 Women Who Shape Our City."

Also by Rolanda T. Pyle

FINALLY - a collection of poetry

Beneath His Everlasting Wings - a devotional

Grandma's Hands - a children's story book.

Connect with Rolanda T. Pyle

Website: http://www.rorosrainbowcommunications.com/

Facebook: https://www.facebook.com/rorosrainbow/

Instagram - https://www.instagram.com/roroscommunications/

Twitter: @RolandaPyle

LinkedIn: https://www.linkedin.com/in/rolanda-pyle-b91ba314

LUISA KAY REYES

The Gracious Bequest

Luisa Kay Reyes has had pieces featured in "The Raven Chronicles", "The Windmill", "The Foliate Oak", "The Eastern Iowa Review", and other literary magazines. Her essay, "Thank You", is the winner of the April 2017 memoir contest of "The Dead Mule School Of Southern Literature". And her Christmas poem was a first place winner in the 16th Annual Stark County District Library Poetry Contest. Additionally, her essay "My Border Crossing" received a Pushcart Prize nomination from the Port Yonder Press. And two of her essays have been nominated for the "Best of the Net" anthology. With one of her essays recently being featured on "The Dirty Spoon" radio hour.

Connect with Luisa Kay Reyes

https://www.amazon.com/Luisa-Kay-Reyes/e/B0786QN9ZR%3Fref=dbs_a_mng_rwt_scns_share

VAUGHN ROSTE

Last Sunday

Vaughn Roste has written books, plays, poems, peer-reviewed articles, book reviews, program notes for CD liners and Carnegie Hall, and a doctoral dissertation, most of which never paid. His book, The Xenophobe's Guide to the Canadians, published by Oval Books in England (1st edition 2003 through the 8th edition, revised, 2016) just went out of print. He recently optioned a screenplay, ORADOUR, a WWII historical drama - for that screenplay and a few other shorts he won 17 screenwriting awards in 2020.

. . .

Connect with Vaughn Roste

Follow him on Twitter @Vaughn09187022

KATHRYN SADAKIERSKI

Bright Nights

Kathryn Sadakierski's writing has appeared in ActiveMuse, Capsule Stories, Critical Read, DoveTales, Halfway Down the Stairs, Literature Today, NewPages Blog, Northern New England Review, Origami Poems Project, seashores: an international journal to share the spirit of haiku, Snapdragon: A Journal of Art and Healing, Teachers of Vision, The Voices Project, Visual Verse, Yellow Arrow Journal, and elsewhere. She graduated summa cum laude with a B.A. from Bay Path University, and is currently pursuing her master's degree. Kathryn lives in New England, where she is very much inspired by the nature and art of the region.

TUFIK Y. SHAYEB

Mr. Robot

The Fifteenth of December

Tufik Y. Shayeb's poetry has appeared in numerous publications, including West Trade Review, Potomac Review, Sheepshead Review, The Menteur, Lost Lake Folk Opera, Madcap Review, Heyday Magazine, Blinders Journal, Muzzle Magazine, and others. To date, he has published three chapbooks and one book titled, I'll Love You to Smithereens. Currently, Shayeb resides in Phoenix, Arizona.

GARY S. WATKINS

A Kiss Under the Mistletoe

Cruel Yule

A fan of fantasy and science fiction for longer than he cares to remember, Gary enjoys putting his own spin on these timeless genres. He has published everything from poetry and micro-fiction to flash fiction and full length short stories. When not writing, he enjoys his daughters and grandkids, tabletop games, karaoke, and getting outside.

Also by Gary S. Watkins

Publications Gary's work has appeared in include: Sirens Call, Star*Line, This Mutant Life: Bad Company, Hex Support, and others.

Connect with Gary S. Watkins

https://www.facebook.com/pseudodragon

LYNN WHITE

Christmas Tree

Lynn White lives in north Wales. Her work is influenced by issues of social justice and events, places and people she has known or imagined. She is especially interested in exploring the boundaries of dream, fantasy and reality. She was shortlisted in the Theatre Cloud 'War Poetry for Today' competition and has been nominated for a Pushcart Prize and a Rhysling Award. Her poetry has appeared in many publications including: Apogee, Firewords, Capsule Stories, Gyroscope Review and So It Goes.

Connect with Lynn White

https://lynnwhitepoetry.blogspot.com

https://www.facebook.com/Lynn-White-Poetry-1603675983213077/

ABOUT THE EDITOR

JK Larkin is a Long Island based writer and recent graduate of Marymount Manhattan College. On top of his position as Literary Manager and Editor of *The Red Penguin Collection*, JK works at The Mary Louis Academy as the coach of their Speech & Debate Team, coaching students to perform excerpts of dramatic literature, prose, and poetry for weekly competitions on both the local and national levels. His body of work draws heavily upon themes of queerness, existentialism, morality, and the struggle to connect in a deeply divided world. This past year, JK published his first two collections, "not kidding." and "Side Street". Follow him at @jksnotkidding on Instagram or @JKLarkinTM on Facebook to keep up to date with his artistic journey.

ALSO FROM THE RED PENGUIN COLLECTION

www.ingramcontent.com/pod-product-compliance
Lightning Source LLC
Chambersburg PA
CBHW030434120726
47903CB00003B/963